THE VISCOUNT'S SON

Rise of the Dark Ones Trilogy – Book One

ADERYN WOOD

Edited by Pam Collings
pam@tbbooks.com.au

Cover Art by Tairelei
www.deviantart.com/tairelei

Cover Stock
www.deviantart.com/dawnallynnstock
www.deviantart.com/castock

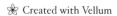 Created with Vellum

To Peter

CHAPTER 1
TO BEGIN

Thursday 1st **August**

    I'm not really sure how to begin. I've never had a blog before, but I used to be on Facebook and I've heard they're similar.

My name is Emma. I work at a very large and famous museum, in a city that is also large and famous. My job entails the conservation, restoration and translation of ancient Latin texts. I'm a book conservator. This may sound as interesting as watching the man who is scrubbing the smog off the workshop window as I write, however, writing about my job, while it will be necessary at times, is not the purpose of this blog.

So I come to the purpose – I wish to translate a book.

On Monday, I overheard a conversation between Jack, a fellow conservator, and our department curator, Monsieur Philippe. They were discussing a book, or more specifically, a diary. When I approached them I overheard "sixteenth century" and my heart leaped. The sixteenth is my favourite, mainly because of the stream of fascinating events and people in that century. It saw the end of the War of the Roses; the reign of Henry VIII and the major bitch fight that followed when his two daughters grappled for the throne. Then there's Shakespeare and Nostradamus (his prophecies are fascinating!). But, this blog isn't about my obsession with English history, so let me get back to the purpose.

When Philippe finally left, Jack let me look at the little book. Not for long enough, though. I was disappointed Jack had got this job rather than me. The fact that the book appeared to be a diary only heightened my disappointment. I longed to know the secrets it held.

I, on the other hand, was stuck with the most tedious job in the museum (aside from cleaning those windows). My current project is just a long process of data entry: listing the soldiers who fought in major European conflicts in the later middle ages. Thankfully, I've only been given the job for British soldiers. The project is called 'The Medieval Soldier Database' and continues the work started by Dr Adrian Bell. I don't deny the significance of the job, but ploughing through reams of various exchequers' records becomes a little monotonous. At least I get to begin with the sixteenth century.

Today, I noticed Jack had put the diary on top of the precariously high 'in' pile on his desk. I was puzzled, as it wore no special jacket to protect it from the atmosphere. In fact, sitting on top of Jack's in-tray offered very little protection from anything. We take a number of precautions when working with ancient texts; they are handled with great care. We normally only place them on the laboratory table to work on or read. When I asked him about it, I was surprised by the answer.

"It's a fake. I don't know how they did it, but they're good!" I remembered his words because they were so unexpected; in my five years here I've never come across an actual 'fake'. When I asked him why he thought it was a fake, he just smirked and said, "Read it, you'll see." Then he handed me the book and told me I could have it. I put the diary in a protective cover and returned to my work for most of the day.

As soon as Jack left, I put my gloves on and took the book to the lab table. It was bound in the usual leather and had remained exceptionally intact. The cover had the letters "N.C." engraved into it. I opened to the first page, which had a single title in Latin – *Anno Mortem Meam*, translated it read - "The Year of my Death".

I couldn't help myself and read on. After skimming most of the book, I understood why Jack assumed it was a fake. Of course a story like that couldn't possibly be true. However, I only translated random segments, and the structure of the book seemed so authentic. In any case, someone had put a lot of effort into it.

So, I have decided to translate the seemingly dark tale this little book tells, and transcribe it in this blog. As a fake it tells a riveting story – but is it a product of the twenty-first century, or the past? I think there is more to it than meets the eye.

Cheers for now,

Emma.

CHAPTER 2
DEAR READER

Friday 9th **August**

This blogging thing is really taking off. I checked my stats today. I have one reader – from Spain. Thank you, whoever you are!

I spent last weekend wishing time would speed up. I was itching to get back to work to do some testing on the diary. Despite the fact that Jack believes it to be a fake, I decided to conduct the usual experiments. Perhaps the testing will support Jack's conclusion. But then again, perhaps not.

At the back of the diary, there are a number of spare pages with no text. I made the decision to sacrifice one of them, and on Monday, carefully cut off a fragment of parchment and sent it to the lab for dating. The results came back today and they do not support Jack's conclusion. The lab report confirms the parchment was made in the first half of the sixteenth century, probably no later than 1530. It is made from sheepskin, which was typical in Western Europe at that time. So, what does this mean? Well, the book itself is an authentic artefact from the sixteenth century.

The parchment and leather that binds it were put together then. Whether the ink on its pages is from the same time is another question. One I hope to investigate. At the moment, I am excited that the pages, at least, are the real deal.

Jack had done no testing on this book; he believed it to be a fake based on the story alone. This was a little unprofessional of him, actually, but, he prides himself on his fast approach, which isn't always a bad thing. I have a habit of spending too much time on a project; at least I know my analysis is thorough.

I have started the translation, and as promised, I will relate its story on this blog. So, here is the first page translated from Latin. It seems to be an introduction to us – the readers. I apologise for any delay in posts. The translation takes time as I want it to make sense to modern day readers, and I have to do all the translating in the lab here at work. An atmosphere anywhere else would cause the text to deteriorate.

Enjoy,

Emma.

First Translation

Dear Reader,

Does the spirit of a man define him? The priests tell us it is so. But what if a man is bereft of his spirit? How is he then to be defined? Does he become free of the temptations of sin? Oh reader, it is not so.

Sin tempts me, like a whore in the finest red silk. It beckons, it calls, it flirts, it teases. I struggle, and yet I am young. I am cursed to exist like this – wild. No longer am I immune to the temptations the darkness offers. Me, a viscount's bastard.

It has been a year since my spirit left me a broken man. I write it down here, now, for what else is there?

Beware, the whore in the night. She takes more than your lust, fool. Heed the warning within these pages and beware.

N.C.

CHAPTER 3
THEY CAME FROM THE EAST

W**ednesday 14th August**

What a week!

Monsieur Philippe, the department curator, has been loitering around the lab lately. He drives me crazy, asking inane questions and trying to exert pressure to hurry things along. The craft of conserving, cataloguing, translating and restoring ancient texts takes time and Philippe's interruptions have done nothing but slow me down. I know Jack feels the same way – we have rolled our eyes frequently at each other.

I am still plodding through the Medieval Soldiers Catalogue, but it is so repetitive. All I really want to do is work on the diary. I have been working on it whenever Philippe is not around, which is not very professional, but I want to get more translation done.

On Monday, when I thought Philippe was at a meeting for an hour, I scraped some ink fibres from a spot on one of those back pages. I knew the parchment was sixteenth century, and I wanted to date the ink.

As I was labelling the sample for testing, Philippe returned and caught me in the act of working on the diary rather than the catalogue. I tried to think of an excuse, but I've never been good at lying. He threw one of his temper tantrums and started muttering about 'professionalism' and 'schedules'.

Then he looked at the diary. He put his hand out and said, "Give it to me." He told me I wasn't to work on the diary at all – that it was a waste of time as Jack had verified it was a fake – and then he left with the diary in his hand!

Philippe's mood swings can make life awkward at work. Sometimes he seems more like an adolescent than a man in his sixties. I think he took the diary out of spite. I'm disappointed. This text has me so intrigued and if I don't get it back, I won't be able to complete the translation. And, according to my blog stats, I now have a small following of readers. Whoever you are, I don't want to disappoint you. I want to see this through to the end.

But, there is some good news. I got the results back from the testing of the ink. It, too, is from the early sixteenth century! I almost hit the ceiling when I read the results. This means the whole text – pages and writing (ink) – date from the early half of the sixteenth century. The story was written then! This is one interesting 'fake'. I just hope I can convince Philippe to give me back the book.

Luckily, I had already translated another section of the text, before the diary was taken from me, and I've shared it below. Let's hope we can complete this story. Just as a matter of interest I thought I'd point out that N.C. used the word 'Aegyptius' in Latin, to describe what I believe we now call 'gypsies', so I have used the term 'gypsy' in the following translation even though 'Aegyptius' actually translates to 'Egyptian'.

Emma.

Second Translation

How far back do I dare take you?

I recall the day the gypsies arrived. They came from the east. I was engaged in the instruction of a group of young squires, practising their footwork in swordplay, a most fundamental skill. I recall this day clearly; it was hot, the sun was a golden fury in a cloudless sky. Now that I remember it, the scent of sunshine lingers nostalgically before me. We tarried in the courtyard of my father's manor; we heard them before we saw them.

The bells and singing of a most foreign group echoed through the heat. Our ears pricked to the aberration. A strange discordance of music and babel flowed from the woodland's path. Then we saw them. A caravan of colour. I had never seen such bold crimson, such gaudy yellow. I leaned on my sword and wiped the sweat from my visage, and what I saw next sent a chill through my heart.

A black carriage, led by a solitary black horse, followed the caravan. It was enclosed completely – no windows. All manner of symbols and pentagrams were painted across it. I recall shivering despite the heat and my hand crossed my heart – a fickle attempt to ward off evil. The dark carriage was ominous. And, now, writing this, I know what it encased. If only I had fled, to be free, to be saved!

CHAPTER 4
THE FAYRE

Thursday 22ˢᵗ August

Last week I buried myself in my work and made some very good progress on the Soldiers Database. Philippe, when he inevitably interrupted, was impressed.

"Emma, you outdo yourself!" I remember him saying.

I tried not to laugh when Jack mimicked Philippe behind his back, hand gestures fluttering, and I'm glad I didn't. Philippe asked me to come to his office at the end of the day. I felt a little nervous. The last time I went to his office he gave me a lecture for taking two weeks on a project that he believed deserved no more than three days.

Having no choice I went, trying not to chew my nails. When I stepped in he seemed surprisingly calm. He asked me to sit down and then he picked up the plastic package – the one I had put the diary in.

"What exactly were you doing with this?" he asked.

I shrugged, trying to appear as casual as possible, even though my heart raced like crazy. I told him I was fascinated by the story it told and it had become a little side project. He sniffed and threw the book across his desk. It landed with a thud and I jumped. He told me not to work on it during work hours.

I picked up the diary and walked out slowly, trying with all my strength to hide the wide grin that spread across my face.

Monday afternoon I went to the department store and bought the best portable air conditioner and humidifier I could afford. If I'm to work on my little project at home I need to get the conditions right, and in the current heat we're having here, it is particularly important. I'm not going to complain about having an air conditioner now. It will make my life, not to mention my sleep, easier, too. Agh, this heat!

I have done a little more of the translation. As soon as I return home from the museum each day, I have been putting the diary on my desk and getting to work – enjoying the new coolness my shoebox apartment offers. There's more talk of the gypsies and things are heating up a little for N.C. I don't want to give anything away, so on to the translation.

Emma.

P.S. I now have a total of eleven regular readers, thank you!

Third Translation

It is summer now and the rich perfume from the rose outside my window wafts relentlessly through my room. The fragrance serves to remind me, more vividly, of the events years afore ...

The gypsies had arrived midsummer, and with them their colour and fare. It was a peaceful time – but peace bodes ill for a soldier. I grew bored of training squires and polishing armour. I was captain then. A position that befitted the bastard status granted me when my father lay with a scullery maid, almost thirty winters past.

My fellow soldiers were also bored with the scant entertainments of a peaceful kingdom. We arranged to visit the gypsy's fayre that evening, to see what sport may be had.

That was when I saw her. That was when everything changed.

We had our fill of ale, and my friends dispersed, each following their own desires.

I noticed a pavilion, somewhat removed from the rest of the fayre. The canvas was painted a dark red and the symbols and pentagrams I had observed on the carriage the day prior, I now witnessed on the surface of the tent. A foreign fragrance filled the air; a spicy rose scent lingered and drew me to the entrance. I heard a voice entreat me – a feminine tone like none I had heard before. I drew the curtain and entered.

The sight before me was exquisite. There were many candles burning brightly and I couldn't help but marvel at the expense of it. Oil burners and incense like those in church lined the interior and a heady scent filled my mind. My eyes adjusted to the light and I saw before me a plethora of treasures. There were gold and silver statues of cats and dogs and many other beasts; some of them had human bodies. Intricate tapestries hung along the sides, and there were woollen rugs on the floor littered with embroidered cushions and pillows.

In the centre of the pavilion was a bed, canopied by a red velvet curtain. My eyes drew quickly to it and the creature that inhabited it as she spoke to me, "Come; don't be afraid."

I pause now, considering this memory, for fear is the precise emotion I should have felt. Rather, I was – aroused. She was, as I say, like no other. Long limbs, bronzed and slender, were exposed between the folds of a sheer, red dress. She wore a corset, the lace tied in a fragile knot at the curve of her breast, a knot so easily unravelled. A red vial on a thin thread hung around her neck, and rested seductively between her breasts. She eyed me playfully and wet her lips; her dark, charcoal eyes scanned my every move.

In the moment it took me to take in this scene, a goblet of dark red wine was pressed into my hand and I was seated at a small table. She moved swiftly to the chair opposite, hand extended, grasping my own. My pulse raced, my head clouded by the fragrance, the wine – her beauty. Her touch felt like ice, but sparks flew to my heart – and my groin – when she turned my hand playfully between her own.

She studied my palm, smiling at me alluringly. I supped the wine as I watched her full lips, my eyes wandering frequently to her neck – her breasts – that knot seemed so easily undone ...

In a moment – one ecstatic moment – she had my fingers in her mouth, kissing, licking, sucking. I felt breathless, my control diminished. I reached for her, but she was quick, so very quick.

She stood, and then turned to me slightly – her body in profile, the candles illuminating the shine of her raven hair upon her breasts. This did little to settle my passion.

A hand – a servant's hand? – guided me from the pavilion. That night I walked in a dream. The minutes were as centuries, for I longed to be with her.

CHAPTER 5
CAUGHT IN A WEB

S unday 25th August

Before I left work on Friday, I received a call from a friend, Amelie, who works in the Impressionists section of the museum. She asked me to go out for some fun. Of course, I was tempted to have a night out. But the diary is far too exciting, so I told Amelie I was too tired, but promised to go out with her soon.

I raced home, stopping briefly at the pizzeria below my apartment to get my Friday night meal – a large slice of margarita. It wasn't long after, that I had the diary on my desk again. With a nice glass of Bordeaux red, I settled in to do another translation. I've spent a large portion of the weekend on it.

What did you think of the last translation? Things certainly heated up for N.C., but if you think that was steamy wait till you read the latest instalment! I have to say, I'm enjoying translating this text more than watching 'True Blood' and I love that show.

In this next section of text, he meets up with the mysterious gypsy woman again. Sorry about the spoiler, but I want to highlight a particular word said by the gypsy. N.C. writes it as 'atimar', but I believe she was probably saying 'atma' which is an ancient Romani word and indeed is still used in some languages, such as Hindi. It loosely translates to 'soul', but because this is my interpretation, I have kept the word as 'atimar' in the translation.

Once again, enjoy!

Emma.

Fourth Translation

Last night I watched a spider entangle a moth in her web. The moth struggled clumsily in the sticky substance. I considered, briefly, the idea of freeing the insect; sometimes compassion arises within me. However, before I could make up my mind, the spider had sprung. She leapt with great agility and speed, and in the instant it takes to blink, she had her victim in her grasp.

The day following my encounter at the fayre remains somewhat of a mirage. I seem to remember polishing a breastplate, the day was hot again, but my mind was focused only on the events of the night before. My thoughts returned relentlessly to the beauty and allure of the gypsy. The scent of the oils, the tone of her voice, the taste of the wine; all the sensual delights from the few moments I was with her were clear and vivid.

I ruminated all day, until a page approached me with a message. I touched the scroll to my lips and breathed the familiar scent of spiced rose. I tore at the red ribbon and my eyes, hungry for information, read the note. It was written in an exquisite hand, the ink red ...

Come to me tonight.
After the moon has waned.

I stared at the words, rereading them, my heart a bolted horse!
The afternoon drifted into evening, and finally into night. I passed the time with my fellows, drinking ale in the tavern, waiting, dreaming ...

Finally, midnight came, and I walked to her tent. Once again, I was struck by the scent of wild, spiced rose. A warm breeze caressed my face and moved the crimson curtains, exposing the lamplight within. I entered.

The pavilion remained exactly as I remembered it, but she sat at the table, waiting expectantly, smiling and gesturing for me to sit. I took the seat opposite, and once again, a goblet of wine was proffered. I looked at the bearer this time and saw a small woman, bent and aged, her eyes blank but friendly. Then she disappeared.

I felt a hand caress my own – the gypsy's hand. Delight took me once again. Her charcoal eyes looked deep into mine and I was filled with an ecstatic pleasure.

"I can see your atimar," she said, her voice deep and alluring.

I was hardly aware of what she was saying, so distracted by her charms. It is only now, on reflection, I see the significance of her words.

"We are all born with atimar," she said, "but some walk without."

Then she had my fingers in her mouth again, and I dropped the goblet. I reached for her as I had done the night before and this time she remained still.

I caressed her neck, and followed the line of her shoulders, then touched the swell of her breasts with the back of my hand. I grasped the knot that held together the red corset she wore. Some great strength overcame me for I tore it apart and the corset fell lose, exposing her full breasts and exquisite beauty.

In another moment, I had her in my arms and carried her to the canopied bed, whereupon I kissed her lips, her throat, her breasts. I remember it well, for such forbidden fruit was laid bare and I gorged myself on it. The ecstasy of that night was like no other. My hands can still feel the form and thrill of her most secret parts.

… Oh, I was entangled, deep within her web!

CHAPTER 6
LOVE BITE

Saturday 21st September

Firstly, I must apologise for my absence. I have been in the field and I believe this work has some link to my translation of N.C.'s diary.

So where have I been? Egypt. Philippe was desperate for a restorer to visit one of our long term digs.

Our museum has a number of partnerships with Egypt and other countries. We have roughly a dozen digs in operation at the moment. My job was to simply ensure the scrolls and canvases found were preserved correctly for transport back here. It took several weeks to clean the pieces and get them ready for transport. Now they are in a lab in the bowels of our museum, being analysed and translated by some lucky person.

I feel so privileged to have seen them. There were a number of art pieces, and scrolls with simple hieroglyphs. It was the art, however, that caught my attention. We believe they tell the story of the nomadic gypsies who moved over the millennia through almost every continent imaginable. The pieces had such brilliant colour, mostly showing the stories of nomadic travel, but a few also conveyed festivals. There were paintings and needlework of large pavilions and tents and one of them, when I looked very closely, had an image of a pentagram. I managed to do some research while I was there and it seems that in Egypt the pentagram was a symbol of the womb of the underground that gave birth to all things evil. The pavilion in one piece was red and it reminded me a little of the one N.C. spoke of.

Of course, it is unlikely to have been the same one; we dated the artefacts from the dig to the thirteenth century.

This diary is so interesting and I am glad to be back so that I can put all my efforts into the translation again. By the way, I asked Philippe where the book came from; he said it came from a site in this very city. It seems there was a fire at an Indian restaurant and in the aftermath, a few old world treasures were found, buried under the site. I wonder how it got there.

I now have 30 regular readers, Thank you!

Enjoy it.

Em.

Fifth Translation

She had me. I was in utter awe of her charms, and they were many. I have frequently pondered on what could have been – if only the gypsies had gone to a different town, if only I had avoided her tent. Such ponderings are useless now of course. Now I am irrevocably changed.

I met with her every night. The moon seemed to remain in a perpetual state of fullness, for each evening it would light my way to her pavilion where the spiced rose perfume drew me in. Our passion had intensity like fire, it raged through the night. I left each dawn, spent.

The days were arduous. The boredom of peacetime rituals did little to stop my mind wandering back to sweet dreams of her.

The last night we were together was most thrilling. She was waiting for me as usual, but, this time there was no preliminary talk, no wine prof-fered. When I entered the red tent, my breathing stopped the very moment I saw her. She knelt on the canopied bed, her arms open awaiting my embrace, gloriously naked. Her womanhood was fully exposed, her perfect, dark hair cascaded down over her ample breasts, the curvature of her waist, the dark patch of hair, glistened in the candlelight. My arousal was immediate.

She enjoyed this, too. She watched me and smiled at the immediacy of my reaction. Her hands gathered her hair up and I watched her graceful movement in wonder. It was too much. I went to her, kissing that slender neck, cupping my hands to her breasts, feeling her exquisite shape, tasting her. Even now I desire her – after all she did ...

In the passion of that night, an erotica was awoken in her that was ecstatic. She sat atop me; I can still see the way she arched her back, moving seductively. I suckled her breast hungrily. She threw herself forward and kissed me fully, my lips, my neck. Her teeth and tongue grazed my skin. It was so pleasurable when it came, a love bite like no other.

The skin of my throat gave way under the piercing bite. It conjured a heat that pulsed through my entire being. It brought me to climax and it was heavenly. She drew back, and I could see the blood on her lips, but it did not frighten me. I was drunk on her lust and like a drunk, I lay back exhausted.

She woke me once, to offer water. I was thirsty and I gulped the cup down. It was dawn when I awoke again and she was not there. I dressed and took my leave.

CHAPTER 7
FEVER

T hursday 26th September

     I'm working double time at the museum. Philippe wants the Egyptian artefacts fully conserved and has put me in charge. Of course, I'm excited by this. I love working with the vibrancy and colour of the gypsy relics, not to mention the historical significance. But Philippe wants me to step up my work with the Medieval Solider Database as well. I don't blame him, I know he has deadlines to meet, but it's so tedious. Really, it's just data entry, anyone could do it; it doesn't require a trained conservator!

So, my life is all work, no play. Amelie keeps nagging me to go out. I used to have a wonderful social life. Out for dinner every Friday and Saturday night, followed by dancing the night away. I need to get my life back. You should see my apartment. I have two mountains in it; and remember I live in a studio. One mountain has my clothes for the laundry; the other has my clean clothes, yet to be put away. They're like a giant 'in-and-out-tray'.

All I really want to do is get stuck into the diary. I haven't had much time for it at all. I have managed to do a little translation, and I've posted that below. I can't wait to translate it entirely.

What did you think about the gypsy? Provocative stuff, huh? Maybe that's why Jack didn't like it. Perhaps it offended his sensibilities. Knowing Jack, I rather doubt it.

Emma.

Sixth Translation

I slumbered all day and when I awoke at dusk, my fatigue had abated little. My exhaustion lay heavy on my shoulders, as though I wore a full suit of armour. I recall dragging my body from my bed and pouring a cup of water. I gulped it down and poured another, it was as sweet as Roman wine. Only then did I realise my thirst, and hunger. I had slept the day away – me, the captain of my father's men. I remember the shame I felt. Interesting, even bastards succumb to the poison of honour.

I called for the squire and instructed him to prepare a cool bath. It was the height of summer and I had fever that burned like fire on my skin.

The boy nodded, but studied me closely. He asked if I was well. I was not. He pointed at my neck and his young face contorted into an expression filled with horror, 'Master, your neck'.

I looked in the glass. My face was white, like winter. An inflamed festering wound pronounced itself on the side of my neck. I touched it gently with my fingers and felt the heat, like coal as it burned. I stumbled but leaned closer, and in the dim dusk light, I studied the welt. There were two puncture wounds. Twin pricks, round, red and sore. I called for the chirurgeon; he came quickly. He bandaged my wound and asked no questions, demanding only that I be bled. I refused.

As night fell, I made my way outside. My pace was slow; the weakness encumbered me like a heavy chain around my neck.

I walked toward the fairground. Even in my fever I was drawn irrevocably back – to her. But when I arrived, there was nothing – the tents, pavilions, the people, the fayre – they were all gone. Only the silver light of the moon and the summer breeze remained. And in that breeze, I perceived the subtle scent of spiced rose ...

CHAPTER 8
DESIRE

S aturday 5th October

Work is finally easing up. I have been allocated an assistant to help with the conservation of the Egyptian artefacts. Jack is helping as well. He asked me how my "little project" was coming along. I haven't told him about this blog – we're not supposed to be so public about the documents we transcribe. But since Philippe has officially labelled the diary a fake, I'm not too worried about it being in the public domain. I was reticent in my reply to Jack, though; he'd view my work on the diary as a waste of time.

The word 'gypsy' seems to be infiltrating my life at the moment. Amelie finally dragged me out for some fun last night. We went to Le Carré for fine dining, and then on to The Gypsy Bar for some dancing. I love that bar. It reminds me of the descriptions of the Gypsy's pavilion in N.C.'s diary. The walls are red with lavishly embossed wallpaper. The lighting is entirely candlelight. It makes me feel as though I've stepped back in time.

After a couple of Frangelicoes on ice, Amelie got me up dancing. A Spanish guitar troupe was playing and when they strummed the opening chords to *Bamboleo* Amelie jumped to her feet. I'm not the best dancer on account of my two left feet, but I loved it. It was wonderful to relax and have fun and just enjoy the music.

Little did I know I was being watched. Amelie and I danced for a handful of songs, and only sat down to rest when the band declared a break. Amelie decided we needed a cocktail and went off to the bar. I sipped my water and watched the crowd milling around our table. That's when I saw him.

A man sat at a shadowy corner table. He swirled a glass of wine. The momentary glow of his cigarette as he inhaled revealed a handsome face, framed in black silk hair, and dark eyes that looked directly at me. I smiled then and looked away. There was something so intense and interesting about him. I got that feeling, you know, when you see someone who attracts you? Like a butterfly sensation in the stomach. I looked around for Amelie; she was still at the bar. When I looked back at the corner table, he was gone.

I was a little disappointed, and started scanning the bar.

I nearly jumped when I heard a deep voice right beside me. "Looking for me?"

I know it sounds cheesy but he really said that. He said a lot of other things too. I think I'm hooked already. We talked for the rest of the night. Luckily, Amelie also found a friend.

So – his name is Nathan. But he prefers Nate. He took my number and he said he would call. I'll let you know what happens.

But, let's get back to our viscount's son.

There's not a lot happening in the next update, and I admit, I shortened the original a little, but I believe we have a definitive year in which the diary was written. In this translation, you'll notice that N.C. mentions a particular legislation, and I believe he was referring to the Egyptians Act of 1530. This law was passed in that year to allow the authorities to physically remove the gypsies, who many considered devious troublemakers. Since N.C. is reflecting over the past year, the diary must have been written in 1531, or not long after anyway. It would certainly fit with the testing I have done.

Enjoy.

Emma.

BTW - I have over 50 followers now!

Seventh Translation

As the days passed I recovered from my lethargy, and the wound on my neck healed. My physical strength was renewed and I returned to my duties as Captain. The summer slowly surrendered. The gardens replaced their scarlet roses with the burnt orange and blood reds of the autumn leaves, and the long nights of winter were quick to follow.

I could not forget the gypsy woman. She returned in my dreams to dance around me wearing a scarlet gauze cape, so fine I could see her nakedness in full. The cape would be tied with a fragile ribbon, but when I reached for it I would wake to find my arm extended before me, grasping for the imagined ribbon.

It was a hard winter. The boredom of peacetime offered no distraction. I wished for summer and the return of the gypsies. But in this, some news arrived that shattered such a wish. The fools who rule from parliament had passed a mandate; they wanted the gypsies expelled. With little in the way of war to occupy the realm's soldiers, we were called upon to enforce the act ourselves. Come summer, I would be faced with a choice. I was divided in two, the soldier who followed orders and the man with a desperate desire for a nameless woman ...

CHAPTER 9
THE RETURN

T
hursday 10th October

I had myself convinced Nate wouldn't call and spent all week reminding myself I'm an adult, not a teenage girl. Of course, I hoped he would call. Yesterday – he did.

I'd just got home from work and had a shower. He called as I was drying my hair.

"Have you been thinking about me?" His deep voice in my ear sparked a hot blush and I was glad he wasn't there to see it. Can you believe his front? I'm sorry about the gushing but this guy is so intriguing. Usually the arrogant types don't get a second look from me, but there's something about Nate that has me. I want to go along for the ride, at least for a little while. I need some fun. I've been working so hard lately.

He invited me out Saturday night. He's going to pick me up at seven. Very traditional.

I think this blog has turned into my personal journal. Some people are reading it regularly (76 readers my stats tell me) but I have no idea who. I like how I can reveal myself anonymously to a group of strangers and no one who reads it will ever really know who I am. I find it liberating somehow. What a world we live in!

I haven't forgotten the whole reason I started this blog in the first place. I am still determined to translate the diary entirely and I have another translation for you below.

I'll post again after my date and I promise to let you know all about it.

Em.

Eighth Translation

Authority means so little now. Back then, it was everything ...
Summer had returned. It was to be my last.

We received word that the gypsies were moving from the east, making their way to us for their summer Fayre. The royal orders arrived promptly. I understood the decree. We were to exterminate them.

I threw the scroll on the fire in my father's chamber. This was not what the law had intended. They were supposed to be moved on, imprisoned at most. Not this. Not murder. "Fix it" was all my father said and he left to attend more pressing matters for a viscount.

With no war, an army had to earn its keep. The King wanted these nomads removed and we were the assassins to do the job. I planned the charge. It would be an easy catch. An ambush. A slaughter.

I played my part, ordering my men, running through the drills. We were ready. The gypsies were due to arrive the following evening.

I could not get her off my mind – her lips, her raven hair, her breasts. I wanted her.

That evening I supped my wine and tasted her. I studied the village maps but saw only her.

I had to do something.

CHAPTER 10
A WARNING

Sunday 13th October

I think I am falling for him. Last night was so – I don't know – perfect? He met me downstairs and we walked to a wine bar close to my apartment. I knew it well, and so did he, which surprised me. To think, in such a large city, I could have sat beside him in that very bar before.

We dined at the Savoy. He had the ox blood soup. I had the escargot – my favourite. The food was exquisite but I had a poor appetite. When I'm around him an electricity pulses through my body, it makes eating difficult. Though it doesn't stop my drinking.

He has the darkest eyes, not that I could hold his gaze. I just glanced at him. My eyes darted around the room all night. Sometimes I'm such a coward!

The conversation was probably not very fluent. He stared at me so intensely for the most part and paid so many 'last century' compliments.

"Your eyes are like emeralds, Emma, so beautiful." "The smoothest ivory could not match your flawless skin."

Can you believe it? Honestly, I feel like a character in a Victorian romance novel. But it's just so – nice, to feel this way. He asked me many questions and seemed particularly interested in my job. I yearned to tell him about this blog and my translation of the diary, but I stopped myself.

He walked me home, and kissed my cheek.

He wants to see me again next Friday night and I honestly don't know how I can wait that long. I'm so glad I have the diary to translate. It will keep my mind busy at least.

When I awoke this morning my head was a little sore from the wine. I called Amelie. She begged me to tell her all about him, which I did. She's caught up in my romance, too.

I did a fair bit of translation today. This story is unbelievable. I just can't figure it. Is the author a storyteller? It is so unlikely for that era. The book itself is a genuine artefact from the sixteenth century, but the story simply can't be true. Perhaps N.C. suffered from mental illness and all of this is a retelling of the strange delusions he experienced. That seems to be the most likely explanation.

Whatever the reason, I am enjoying the unravelling and I look forward to the end. I would like to try to investigate more about our mysterious N.C. Who was he exactly? Most likely, I will never find out, but maybe I should try.

I will post again through the week with another translation. Enjoy!

Emma.

Ninth Translation

The moon was full and at its zenith. I rode hard. I had to warn her. I had to see her.

Their camp was easy to find and the red pavilion stood a little apart from the rest. I tied up my horse in the woodland and made the short journey to her on foot. But when I got there a man, his arms folded across his black embroidered vest, greeted me.

"She not here." He told me. "She sends message."

He handed me a small scroll and when I touched it to my nose the familiar scent of spiced rose filled my nostrils.

> *Ride back.*
> *Do what your King commands of you.*
> *We will not be defeated.*

I threw the note aside and asked him to summon her. He told me she would not return before the dawn. I tried to warn him then, to turn back, that ahead meant certain death for him and his troupe. He laughed, saying his people had traversed the world for many centuries, and did I really think a small group of bored soldiers could stop them?

I turned to go. "You have been warned," I said.

Again he laughed.

I sped back through the night, and cursed the pride of men. At dawn, I galloped down the road toward my village. As the early morning sky turned purple, I met a carriage on the way and recognised the farmer – one of my father's vassals. Panic danced in his eyes.

"My son," he said, "he has been injured." He opened the curtains of the carriage to reveal the prostrate young man.

"Look to the neck." He told me. And I saw the angry welt, identical to the one I had received the summer before. Twin pricks – red, swollen, sore.

I slammed the curtains shut, mounted, and spurred my horse on. I had little concern for the youth. My anger stemmed from my jealousy. How stupid I had been. Did I think she loved me?

CHAPTER 11
THEY CAME AT DUSK

W ednesday 16th October

As I predicted, this week has dragged. It's been difficult to concentrate on work. I find myself thinking only of him – his dark eyes, his black hair. All this brooding has made me realise how little I know about him. I don't even know his surname! He spent so much of our conversation talking about me, asking me questions. It's so refreshing in a man, but I must learn more about him. I wonder what he does for a living.

I think Jack has twigged that something is going on. He caught me staring out the window today with my hands resting on the computer keyboard. Not doing anything, just staring. I don't know how many times he had to call my name before I answered.

"Are you in love, Emma?" he asked. I apologised and he tried to prise out of me who 'the lucky guy' was, but I don't want to tell him. Not yet.

Still, his question haunts me a little. Am I in love?

This afternoon some red roses were delivered to my work place. The card said only: 'I'm thinking of you'. I blushed. Jack decided I was definitely in love.

I have the roses in a vase now. They are sitting on my desk in my apartment, and I can smell their delicious scent as I write this. Roses these days usually have no aroma whatsoever. But these fill my whole apartment with their rich perfume. I am reminded of the 'spiced rose' N.C. speaks of in the diary.

I have more of the translation for you below. Things really start to get weird now as you will see. On the weekend I'll do more translating, and I promise to tell all about my night with Nate.

Em.

Tenth translation
_____

They came at dusk. We waited in ambush. We lined the woods on both sides of the road that lead to the village. Two lines of soldiers. Snakes ready to spring.

The gypsy troupe moved slowly, like a large snail. They carried all their worldly possessions in their carriages. Some of the children played games alongside the caravan. I crossed my heart. Was I to be forgiven for the killing of innocents?

My men awaited my signal. We barely breathed. I recognised the man who led the column. He wore the same black embroidered vest. He rode a horse at the front and set their slow pace. He was their leader, they trusted him, but he was leading them all to their death.

When he reached the predetermined point in the road I gave the signal and my men rushed out. Silently, solemnly they followed my orders and began the drill. The snakes struck.

In the growing darkness the sounds of screams and drawn steel pervaded the night. I, too, had a job to do. I rode to the leader and raised my sword. Recognition glinted in his eyes, but no fear. It confused me, his calmness. Why did he not shout? Why not run? The screams ensued around me and I assumed my men carried out the order.

But then something registered.

They were the cries of my men. Not the gypsies. What was happening?

My head turned from my target to the scene around me. Something had attacked my men. One by one they cried out in anguish before falling to the ground like soft toy soldiers – lifeless.

I saw her then. Her dark hair flowed freely in the night breeze. The velvet red of her skirts contrasted the blue of the night. Her blouse had been torn open, her breasts exposed and the thin vial swung as she walked toward me. In the rising of the moon, I saw the cruel red line of a sword's slice drawn across her chest. Blood ran down her breasts and glistened in the moonlight. Confusion reigned, but she smiled and continued toward me.

What she did next both perplexed and aroused me.

She took a finger and ran it across her breasts, touching both nipples and covering her finger in the blood. She raised her hand and put her blood-drenched finger in her mouth where she sucked the mortal substance clean off.

She came closer, then. Blood covered her arms like silk gloves. Scarlet droplets were cast across her face and hair. Her eyes burned a coal red and held me in a trance. The screaming around me subsided, and there was movement. The gypsies were on their way again. The children resumed their play and laughed as my men lay on the ground – soldiers dying in the moonlight.

She put her hand around my head and kissed me hard. I thought my desire would burst but I retained control. She brought my head down to her breast and I suckled her nipple, her hot blood filled my mouth and it was sweet.

That's when it came. That bite, sweeter than any prior. Oh, the ecstasy, the joy she brought when her teeth struck hard into my neck. This time she drank my life away, and when she had her fill, she let me collapse to the ground where she mounted me and rocked back and forth pleasuring herself as she rode. When she was done she brought my mouth back to her breast and I drank my fill of her hot lustful blood.

CHAPTER 12
DARKNESS

Thursday 17ᵗʰ October

SEE WHAT I MEAN BY WEIRD? BUT ISN'T IT INTRIGUING? NOT to mention sexy! Makes me look forward to Friday night if you know what I mean. (Did I actually just write that? This blog is so liberating!).

Only one more sleep until my date. I just now got home from shopping with Amelie, who decided I needed something 'chic' for tomorrow night. But I worked out when Amelie says 'chic', she actually means 'sexy'. At first I wasn't sure, but what the hell? In an earlier post I mentioned I just wanted to go along for the ride with this guy, have some fun. "That means lots of sex," Amelie told me. I laughed, but she's right of course. Dead right.

So I lashed out and bought some very sexy lingerie – the see-through lace stuff. Amelie insisted on this little black dress – low-cut, front and back.

"He won't need to take the dress off to see the underwear," I joked.

She just winked and said, "That's the whole point."

Let me cool my head here a minute and I'll inform you of an interesting thing I found out today.

I think I know who N.C. is!

After finally finishing work on the soldiers' database, something twigged. I remembered entering data about some sort of rebellion in the early sixteenth century. I worked on that century first, but after reading back through the catalogue I found it.

In a region called Herefordshire in England, there is evidence of a rebellion that occurred between peasants and soldiers. When I looked through the names of the soldiers present, one name stuck out. His initials struck me at once; his name was Nathaniel Chartley, a captain.

I was stunned. I was so tempted to tell Jack, but I can't tell anyone about this. I couldn't wait to get home tonight to tell you (my anonymous readers).

Now that we've found our mysterious N.C., I've got to learn more about him. I've even thought about taking time off work to investigate him further.

Wish me luck for tomorrow night!

Em.

Eleventh Translation

It was an itch that woke me. Some irritation. I lifted my hand and learned of my entrapment. I opened my eyes. Darkness enfolded me. My hands felt the trap within which I lay. A coffin. A simple wooden box befitting my bastard status. Panic followed confusion.

As ludicrous as it sounds, I feared death. Frantic, my fingers searched for a miracle, but the rough pine box offered no escape. I gulped mouthfuls of air in panic.

Soon enough I learned of my immunity to suffocation, and calmed.

How long did I linger there? Days? Weeks?

One night an urge, a new instinct drove me out. My arms punched upwards and broke the wood as though ripping through parchment. The earth fell inwards but I swam through – up, up, until I broke free and the night air enclosed me. I emerged from the earth a new being, marvelling from a strength previously unknown.

I stood in the graveyard of my village. The moon had waned; it was the depth of night.

As I stumbled through the familiar laneways and fields of my homeland, I looked for the gypsies. There was not a sign of them. Was it all a dream?

CHAPTER 13
THE FIRST BITE

Saturday 19th October

That was the single most memorable night of my life. We dined at Le Meurice. I've never dreamed of going there. The expense is simply beyond me, and the waiting lists are well renowned. He didn't tell me how he managed it. Somehow I think Nate can do whatever he pleases. He can certainly bend me to his will (read on!).

Sitting in that ornate restaurant surrounded by relics from the seventeenth century, I felt as though I really was in another world. The meal was exquisite and we shared the most delicious vintage. I made an attempt to get to know more about him, but he protested; he wanted to learn more about me.

But I persisted. He told me his surname, Smith. So ordinary for such an extraordinary man. I'm more than a little suspicious about that. I tried to press him further about his job, where he came from, but he took my hands, looked at me and said, "Let's get back to you."

Later, we danced – slow, and close. I saw desire deep within his eyes. Everything else peeled away as we moved to the music. The urgency in his eyes deepened and at one point he pushed me away, excusing himself. I took my seat and waited for him to return from the bathroom, my desire just as strong.

When he returned, he apologised and took my hand again. I whispered in his ear that he should come back to my place. Can you believe it?

"You're quite sure?" he asked. I smiled and told him I was.

"I'm ravenous," his lips just touched my ear and I melted.

Instead of going back to my apartment, he led us to a suite he had booked above the restaurant. It was equally as opulent as the restaurant had been. I marvelled at the crystal chandelier hanging low over the mahogany dining table. It was breathtaking.

What can I say about his lovemaking? Let me tell you: he wanted the control and I let him have it. I knew it was going to be the ride of my life. I'd never experienced sex like it and it left me yearning for more.

He peeled the dress from my body and laid me on that splendid table and told me, "I want to taste all of you." And he did. His lips, his tongue caressed every part of my body; his teeth gently grazed my skin and I was in ecstasy.

If I was to tell you any more of the details this blog would get severely sordid!

Finally, as dawn approached, he let me sleep.

I woke at midday to find a single rose beside me in the large hotel bed. The note read: 'I'll come back for seconds soon'. I showered and dressed and took the subway home. All day I have floated in a dream. I cannot wait to see him again.

This afternoon I translated more of the diary (after a detailed phone call to Amelie). It is the only thing that can keep my mind from him.

So, our 'N.C.' hasn't mentioned the 'V' word but we all know what he has become in this story he has weaved. Nathaniel Chartley. I think I will see about taking that leave from work. I haven't had a vacation in a long time and the idea of researching this man is really exciting. Although, I might just stay on this wild ride with Nate for a while longer.

Em.

Twelfth Translation

I walked the King's road that leads out of my village. Dawn fast approached and a great hunger arose within me.

I staggered to a farmhouse. A milkmaid walked toward me, her hand clutching a pail. The cows panicked and moved away, no doubt sensing the monster that lurked too close. The girl tried in vain to control them. I eyed her in the darkness, the way a wolf spies its prey. She was plump, white, innocent. When she saw me her eyes widened in fear and it thrilled me. I wanted her to scream. I reached for her and she ran. The thrill of the chase exhilarated me.

I had her in a few quick paces. My speed and strength were superior. She struggled in my arms, but I held her still and marvelled at the gleam of her milky white throat in the moonlight. I can still remember her scent of butter, youth and sweetness.

My vision blurred, then sharpened, and all at once I could see the red hue of blood, pulsing beneath her translucent skin. My face contorted, involuntarily, and in a blink my teeth had transformed to razor incisors that grazed my tongue. My hand caressed her throat and I noticed the blue veins of my wrist against the white of my own skin. I was changing some-how, but I took it in with a mere casual interest. I was subject to a more instinctual, primal urge – hunger.

The girl struggled again and her pulse quickened, her heartbeat thrummed in my ear. I could resist no longer. My lips curled back and I sank my teeth into her warm flesh and tasted the salty sweetness of my first bite. The forbidden fruit of our age. I was now permanently cast from the Garden of Eden to live a life of death. Trapped in darkness for eternity.

CHAPTER 14
GUILT

F riday 25th October

When I started this blog the intention was to simply translate and discuss the diary, but it has turned into so much more. You, my anonymous readers, are the ones to whom I can reveal all my secrets.

I have fallen in love with Nate. It's more than the thrill ride it once was. If love is all-consuming, as many say it is, then I am completely absorbed.

It's only been three weeks since I first met him, but I feel as though I've known him all my life. I trust him. Last night, we strolled along the river. It was beautiful – the gold and rust colour of the autumn leaves reflecting on the water of the riverbank. We walked arm in arm, my smile broadening with every step. Love is the best feeling!

I told him about this blog. He said he looked forward to reading it. Are you reading it now, Nate?

My heart is pounding in my chest as I write. The only one who truly knows the author of this blog is also my lover.

The diary is almost translated in full. I haven't decided if I will continue this blog once it's done.

We are meeting again tomorrow night. You can tell me what you think then, Nate.

Love,

Emma.

Thirteenth Translation

The monster within was brutal and restless in those first few months. I could not remain in the village; I had left too many victims in my wake. With every – feed, I travelled further south, until gradually I arrived here, in London.

After every kill – in every town and village – I looked for her. The gypsy from whom I inherited this affliction. But as yet, she has remained unseen.

What I would say to her, do to her, when I see her again – I do not know. But the desire overwhelms me. We must reunite. There are questions that demand answers.

I seemed to have acquired powers of the mind. Last night I persuaded a noble woman to come back with me to the basement. She came easily, trustingly. I fed on her, of course.

Upon my arrival, I took up residence in the basement of an inn. The inn-keep refused me at first, but I looked him in the eye and beguiled him easily. My room is nestled deep within the ground, and shields me from the fire of the sun. Near the high ceiling, are two small windows, beyond them grows a rose garden and every night I take comfort in its perfume.

I have acquired other powers too. At times, when I concentrate, I hear the private thoughts of a person's mind, if they are close. It comes to me in a series of images and disjointed phrases. My strength and speed continue to grow. I have jumped to the roof of a house, and scaled stone walls just as a lizard does. With each new victim, it seems I discover some new power.

Am I the devil? My morality is weak. My sense of right and wrong, good and evil, is no longer as clear as it once was. But when I am sated, when the blood rush has worn off, that is when morality returns and overwhelms me.

CHAPTER 15
A SHIP IN THE NIGHT

S unday 3rd November

We didn't speak of this blog, but I know he has read it. Last night we lit candles and he burned some incense. It was delightful and the only way I could think to describe the scent was 'spiced rose'. He smiled and arched his eyebrows a little when I told him this. I knew we both understood the reference.

I'm always under a spell with Nate. But, this time, in the height of our passion, he took my neck in his hands and kissed. I felt a sharp pressure and an ecstasy awoke within me as the hot thread of my own blood worked its way down my chest. He had it all over his mouth too. His eyes usually so dark seemed reddish in the candlelight, like rubies, and more desirous than ever.

In our passion the love bite didn't hurt a bit, rather it added to the lustful sensation that overcomes me whenever he is around.

I know I shouldn't be accepting this. But I feel sure we will do it again. Our lovemaking has gone to another level and I think it will be impossible to turn back now. We are both aware of this blog, but neither of us mention it when we are together. I know he is inflamed by the sensuality that I put into the translations and inspired by the gypsy woman. I am equally enthralled and the ride I am on now seems more dangerous and even more enticing than before. Where will it end?

I now come to the final translation of the diary. I'm not convinced Nathaniel meant for this to be his last entry, it certainly doesn't read that way. But, with this last translation, his words do come to an end.

Nathaniel. Nate is short for Nathaniel. Sometimes when we are making love, I shut my eyes and imagine Nathaniel ...

I think I will blog again to tell you more about this modern-day Nathaniel. It's not over yet.

Em.

Final Translation.

The summer has now returned to its height and I grow restless. My routine of feeding, sleeping and grieving becomes tedious. I want answers to the many questions that flood my mind each evening when I awake from darkness. I must find her.

I have made the arrangements.

In my short time here I have – hunted only nobles. They offer more than blood and I have collected quite the assortment of pretty, fat purses. I leave tonight by ship to France. The gypsies will not return this summer. I am sure of it. I will make my way east and find her. In finding her, will I find peace?

That is what I pray for. But are my prayers still heard?

CHAPTER 16
A TERRIBLE FEELING

Saturday 9th November

    I think it's time the ride came to an end.

I awoke this morning to a blistering wound on my neck and when I inspected closely there were two red punctures festering on my skin. Surely this is coincidence. I am so very weak and tired. My face in the mirror resembles a white sheet. It seems as though I write my own version of the viscount son's diary. What is happening to me?

Nate called. He wants to see me tonight. I didn't answer the phone, letting it go to voicemail instead. I can't see him. I need to rest. I need to return to my normal life. I need to go shopping with Amelie, and joke with Jack, and argue with Philippe about schedules at work.

But I have the most terrible feeling that I will see him tonight. And if that happens, what else will come?

CHAPTER 17
DEAR READER

S unday 10th November

Dear Reader,

She has gone. It was done last night and I think, reader, you know what this means.

The return of my diary and the delights offered by this sensuous young woman provided me with a distraction from the long nights of tedium I have come to endure.

I came across her quite by accident. I was in Spain at the time, and had just acquired my first iPad. Technology really is a wonder. If only you twenty-first century citizens truly knew how much the world has changed.

Sitting in a bar in Barcelona, I recall reading the latest post on one of the blogs I follow. Feeling curious, I clicked on the 'next blog' link and Emma's blog appeared before me. I recognised it at once – my diary. Her translations were incredibly accurate.

Within a week I had returned here to Paris.

I first came here after leaving England in 1531, when I took up residence in a humble apartment (centuries later, it became an Indian restaurant). I must have forgotten all about the diary then.

It's not surprising; I had much to learn. I've been all over the globe since. Every inch of Earth has been traversed by my footsteps. I have learned much, but still I have questions.

Finding her was easy. Her company – a breath of sweet air. Emma filled the darkness with some short pleasure. I sit at her writing desk, in her apartment, now. The whole room speaks of Emma. Such an innocent yet intelligent woman. She lived in the past – I can see that. Novels line the wall, stories from another era. Jane Austen and the Brontes, in particular. Good fun – the early 19th. So outwardly proper, but scratch the surface ... Yes, I enjoyed that era.

One book on her shelf catches my eye. Perhaps she should have studied it a little more than the others. I remember Stoker well; he knew what the darkness could wreak.

Emma's words, within this blog, have given me a fire that I've not experienced in ages. She reminded me of my original quest – to find the gypsy. Did I ever find her? No. That elusive pursuit died some three centuries ago.

I had quite forgotten about her, my maker, and now I intend to resume that old quest. To find her. The Gypsy. Only she has the answers to my questions.

I will go to Egypt. That old realm holds the key. Emma revealed that much to me and I am grateful for it. Perhaps she will join me, when, or if she wakes. Not everyone inflicted does awake. This much I have learned.

So reader, I shall leave it to you to decide the veracity of this journal. Whether you believe or not is no concern of mine. Indeed, you would do better to simply click off the page and go on with your dreary life. For knowledge of this is dangerous, as Emma would now attest.

Nathaniel Chartley (Nate)

A Viscount's son

. . .

TO BE CONTINUED.

WANT TO LEARN WHAT HAPPENS NEXT?

Did you enjoy *The Viscount's Son*? Why not help spread the word about this unholy trilogy by posting a quick review on Amazon and/or Goodreads.

Want to learn what becomes of Emma? Go find out right now by grabbing a copy of Book Two, *The Earl's Daughter*. Or keep reading below – the first three chapters of Book Two of the *Rise of the Dark Ones trilogy* is included here.

If you'd like to discover other books I've published, check out my catalogue on Amazon.

Finally, if you're interested in finding out more about my writing, and what I'm working on next, sign up to my monthly-ish newsletter to get exclusive news (and treats) about upcoming books.

Happy reading!

Aderyn.

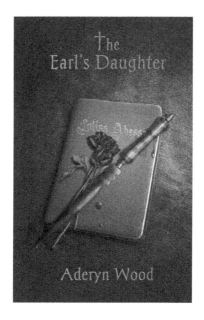

THE EARL'S DAUGHTER

Chapter One

EMAIL FROM LADY SUSAN FARLEIGH - MONDAY 10TH November

DEAR MR D'ANGELO,

Thank you for agreeing to meet. I have convinced my father that you may be able to help us. It has now been a year since Emma's disappearance.

This Saturday would be convenient. Shall we say 10:30? Anyone in town will give you directions to Farleigh House.

Best, Susan.

MICHAEL CREATED A NEW FOLDER TITLED 'EMMA FARLEIGH' and moved the message intoit, before putting the tablet into his coat pocket. He peered through the train window. Fine streaks of drizzle raced down the glass, smudged pretty stone cottages dotting the landscape. Busy streets replaced country lanes as the train drew closer to Wolston.

Lady Susan's email was brief. She'd been short on the phone, too. Her sister had gone missing, kidnapped probably. That was all she told him. He'd questioned her about why she wanted to hire him, surely it was a matter for the police, but she grew more reticent then, saying only that the police could not find her sister, and she had reason to believe that powers more "out of the ordinary" were at play. She refused to elaborate. *Not on the phone,* she'd said. That was the way of the aristocracy.

Michael remembered a case two years ago; Lady Victoria Caraway had a 'presence' in her attic. She'd been more concerned about scandal than any haunting. She even told her butler that Michael was simply a tradesman. That Michael looked more like – well, a priest – than a man who dealt in pipes and effluence didn't deter her. But the butler didn't blink.

The Farleighs sat even further up the chain of nobility than Lady Victoria. Susan's father was Lord Edward Farleigh, the Earl of Wolston. They had even attended royal weddings. Two days ago, while waiting for a haircut, Michael had flipped through an old magazine and seen the pictures for himself. Lady Susan was very attractive; his eyes kept returning to her mass of dark curls and her smile. Her father seemed stern with his deep frown. There'd been no pictures of Emma.

The train pulled in to Wolston Station and Michael strode through the drizzle to the taxi rank, pulling his coat tight. The icy air numbed his nose. He waved to the sole cab but a young lady jumped in front of him. He opened the door for her and waited in the cold, watching the taxi drive off and hoping the next one wasn't too far away.

You're too nice, Michael. A familiar voice came up from a dark well of memory, and Michael pushed it right back down again. He took off his spectacles and cleaned away the drizzle with a handkerchief. Another taxi pulled up and he opened the door before it stopped; he could drop the 'nice' when he wanted to.

"Good morning," Michael said.

The driver nodded absently as he turned down the stereo and Michael was glad. High-pitched nasal Hindi was not a musical favourite.

"Could you take me to Farleigh House?"

The driver's eyes quizzed him in the mirror. "The big mansion on the hill?"

"Ah, I think so. It's where the earl lives." Michael wondered if he should do a search on his phone, but the driver was fingering his GPS and in another second the taxi pulled out onto the road, cutting off a car. Michael took a sharp breath, remembering why he hated taxis.

It took twenty minutes and two near collisions before they pulled up beside a tall stone wall. Michael paid his fare and thanked the driver who turned up his Hindi pop song. The singing faded as the taxi accelerated into the drizzle.

Michael buttoned his coat, wishing he had worn a scarf. A large iron gate stood before him, a vast manicured garden beyond. A hedge-lined path led to the house. The cab driver had been right. It was a mansion, almost a castle. He eyed a turret in the grey skyline, and beneath it stood a small family chapel. He wondered if the Farleighs were religious. Would they know about his past?

"Michael?"

He jumped and glanced around, feeling a little foolish when he saw an electronic speaker near the gate.

"Michael, it's Susan." She was laughing. A camera glared at him, just above the speaker; no doubt she'd seen him jump.

Michael's face warmed. "Ah, hello? Yes, I'm Michael D'Angelo. I'm a little late. I'm sorry. I had to wait for a taxi and—"

"You need to push the button. I can't hear you otherwise." More laughing.

Michael squinted. There was a large white button next to the speaker. "Idiot," he whispered to himself and pushed it. "Hello?"

"That's it. Take the path to the right." With a beep the gates groaned open. "I'll meet you at the side entrance in a jiffy. It's just past the conservatory." She clicked off. He lifted his finger and wiped it on his coat.

Inside the gates he took the path to the right, his shoes crunching wet pebbles. Large elms and oaks lined the pathway, all naked now that autumn was nearly over. After a minute, the conservatory came into view. White wrought iron framed clear glass panels. Orchids and other exotics flowered inside. It would have been added to the house in the Victorian era, no doubt. Conservatories had been all the rage then. The chapel stood to the left of it. Michael adjusted his glasses. The little building seemed older than the rest of the house.

Its dark stone was almost black. Menacing gargoyles with pointed teeth and ears lined the roof. His fingers tingled and Michael wondered if the chapel had something to do with why he was here, rather than the police, or a private investigator.

He would have liked to walk over to it, just to confirm that tingling. But he was already late and a little nervous. Aristocrats made his stomach squirm. Especially the females.

He patted down the cowlick at the back of his head. It gave him a perpetual look of 'bed-headedness' he'd been told. She'd told him that. Judith. He frowned. It was the second time she'd popped out of his hidden memory vault that day. He pushed her back down and closed the lid, wishing he could lock the bloody thing and throw away the key.

A large white door marked the side entrance of the house. He raised his arm, but the door flung open before his hand met wood.

"Michael, hello. Come in out of the weather."

Susan looked exactly as she had in the magazine. Even with all the makeup, she was a natural beauty. Porcelain skin, raven hair, all the right curves. She wore a classic fifties style dress, white with a red floral print. A thin belt showed off her slim waist and a well proportioned bust. He swallowed, muttered "thank you" and stepped inside.

"Can I take your coat? It's too bloody warm in here. My father insists on having all the heating on. Refuses to admit he's getting old," she whispered.

"I see," Michael replied, not really seeing, but wanting to be polite and not say anything stupid like he normally did when in the presence of attractive women.

"So, can I?" she asked. "I'm sorry, can you what?"

"Take your coat?" She smiled, revealing perfect white teeth.

"Of course, my coat. Yes, please." Michael took it off and handed it to his host, wishing again that he wasn't such a natural-born dullard.

She put the coat in a closet then stepped into the hall. "Please follow me. My father is waiting in the library."

Michael obliged, marvelling at the mix of old treasures decorating the place – portraits mostly. Susan's perfume wafted behind her as she walked; a light floral scent that made him think of spring. He liked it.

"Father has not taken my sister's disappearance well." "Understandable," Michael said. "It would be difficult for any parent." "Yes, but he is often reluctant to talk about it, you see."

"Are you sure he wants me to get involved?"

Susan slumped a little, distorting the perfect line of her shoulders. "It was my idea to hire you."

"I see." Michael looked to the marbled floor.

"I heard about you through a friend." Susan reached out and touched his arm. "A Catholic friend."

Michael's face warmed. So, she knew about that. "Well, let's meet your father."

"Daddy, this is Michael D'Angelo. Michael, this is my father – Ted."

The earl wore typical old British tweed and a frown. The same one he'd worn in the magazine. He would have been handsome, in his youth, but age now lined his face.

Michael stepped forward and held out his hand. A pause stalled them, just long enough to make Michael feel even more awkward, before the earl finally took his hand.

"My daughter tells me you are a priest."

"Ex-priest." So, they'd got to that already. The English were so blatant in their distaste of Catholics.

"Oh?" The earl put a hand in his pocket. "Ah, yes. I left the church five years ago."

The earl looked him over with a flick of his eyes. Was it satis-faction or disdain on his face?

"Your name, it is Italian."

"My father was Italian. My mother, Irish."

"Hmph. Little wonder you became a priest."

Susan laughed, a little forcefully. "Now, Daddy, we didn't invite Michael here to interrogate him. Shall we sit?" She gestured to the leather couch and they both sat. The earl remained standing by the window.

Portraits and shelves of books lined the library from floor to ceiling. A lazy fire burned in the fireplace, adding its warmth to the central heating. Michael pulled at his collar, glad that Susan had taken his coat.

"Well, Daddy, shall you tell it or I?"

The earl's mouth drooped a little more; he turned to look out the window.

Susan sighed. "My little sister, Emma, was a conservator, and a good one. She had a situation at the Louvre in Paris."

The earl tutted.

Susan looked at his back, frowning a little and continued. "Daddy didn't want her to take the position."

"She had a perfectly good job at the British Museum," the earl interrupted.

Susan smiled. "Em was enamoured by France. She loved everything about it – the food, the language, the culture."

"Pity about the bloody people."

"Daddy, please! We don't want to waste Michael's time. Now let me tell him so he can help us."

The earl sniffed, straightening his shoulders.

"Just over a year ago, Emma disappeared." Susan's voice wavered. "The police in Paris investigated for a month, then retired the case. Their evidence ran cold."

"Their funding more like."

Susan pursed her lips and gave her father a stare like a parent waiting patiently for a tantrum to finish.

"Their evidence?" Michael asked.

"She was seeing a man called Nathaniel Chartley. She didn't mention him to us, we knew nothing about him. She had a good friend in Paris, Anais, who knew of him, but very little."

"You suspect him of – something?" Michael adjusted his glasses. It seemed more and more to him that the family should hire a private investigator to deal with this. He would hear the rest of the story then delicately suggest it.

Susan looked down at her hands curled in her lap. "My sister has always been a quiet girl. As a child, she was happiest playing by herself, or reading. We used to holiday with our cousins – I'd love that, having more children to play with and boss around."

Susan looked up and smiled, but her eyes were glossy and pink. "But Em was always sneaking off somewhere. We'd find her in the tree house with her nose stuck in a book, more often than not. She's grown into an independent woman now of course. She loves a good time with friends and family, don't get me wrong. But there's still something fragile about Em. Daddy and I have always looked out for her, especially since mother passed away. That was eight years ago. Emma was twenty then, still studying. She took it hard." Susan wiped an eye with a finger, smearing a thin line of mascara.

Michael glanced at the earl. His shoulders were slouched now.

"She was a good girl. Sensible," Susan continued, "but prone to dreaming. Perhaps her curiosity got the better of her. The police found her computer and discovered a strange blog."

Michael squirmed. The case intrigued him, but he still failed to see how he could help.

"The blog detailed a secret quest she had embarked on. She'd come across an old artefact – a sixteenth century journal. One of her co-workers at the museum said it was a fake, but Emma decided to investigate for herself. For some strange reason she set up an anonymous blog to tell of her findings. As she translated the journal, the blog became more personal."

"She wrote about her life?"

Susan nodded. "She changed the names of the people she worked with, but she didn't change her own name. It sounds strange, I know, but I am not surprised. Emma loves a good story, especially a mystery. I think she thought it was a bit of fun."

"And you think the blog and the old diary are connected to her disappearance?" "Yes. You see in the blog she claimed the diary was not a fake. It was a genuine sixteenth century manuscript. And the man she was seeing, Nathaniel – well," Susan looked up, "he was the man who wrote the diary."

Michael frowned. There was no smile on Susan's face now. "But that's impossible."

"We know." The earl turned from the window to look at them. "Show him, Susan. Everything he needs to know." He looked Michael in the eye. "Find out what kind of monster he is, and bring my daughter back to us." The earl nodded, then marched out, leaving Susan and Michael alone.

· · ·

CHAPTER TWO

EXTRACT FROM EMMA'S BLOG — THE VISCOUNT'S SON (First Entry)

MY NAME IS EMMA. I WORK AT A VERY LARGE AND FAMOUS museum, in a city that is also large and famous. My job entails the conservation, restoration and translation of ancient Latin texts. I'm a book conservator. This may sound as interesting as watching the man who is scrubbing the smog off the workshop window as I write, however, writing about my job, while it will be necessary at times, is not the purpose of this blog.

So I come to the purpose – I wish to translate a book ...

MICHAEL SAT ON THE HARD WOODEN SEAT IN THE FOYER OF THE *Police Judiciaire de Paris*. He flipped through Emma's blog entries on his tablet as he waited. The police had accessed the blog during their investigation and made it private, but Susan had asked them not to take it down. Susan provided him with the password and sent him an offline version of the blog along with other documents detailing all the evidence. There wasn't a lot.

Emma Farleigh disappeared after becoming romantically involved with a man called Nathaniel Chartley. In her blog, she revealed Nathaniel was the same man who had written the sixteenth century diary she'd translated. It was impossible of course. And that's why Michael had to take the case.

"Find out what kind of monster he is," the earl had said. But *what* was Nathaniel? Michael didn't jump to conclusions. There was every chance Nathaniel didn't even exist. But Michael had encountered a number of extraordinary things in his life, particu-

larly in his short career as a P.I. He had 'P.I.' printed on his business cards. People thought it stood for 'Private Investigator', but he used 'Private' and 'Paranormal' interchangeably, depending on whom he was speaking with. Most people denied the existence of ghosts and gremlins, and Michael understood why. He often wished he could deny them too.

Vampire.

That word frequented his thoughts now. Hardly surprising given the content of Emma's blog. He didn't deny their existence, he didn't deny anything, but he'd never had a case that dealt with them. He'd never even heard of them outside the stories that recurred in popular culture. Although something tugged at his memory.

"Monsieur D'Angelo?"

Michael snapped his tablet cover shut and looked up to see a middle-aged policewoman – slim, with a stony-faced look, and dark hair pulled back in a tight bun.

"Ah, *bonjour, Madame. Je suis ici pour voir Inspecteur Roulier.*" Michael stood as he summoned his best French; so far it had enabled him to order a hotel room and warm meals, but the Parisians seemed less than impressed. If only the case had taken him to Rome. His Italian was near perfect.

"Inspecteur Roulier is busy," she replied in flawless English. "I am Detective Schleck. I assisted the Inspecteur on the Emma Farleigh case." She glanced at her watch. "Please follow me."

"Ah, *merci beaucoup.*" Michael had to walk double time to keep up with Detective Schleck. The sound of her square heels rang through the high halls of the police headquarters. Michael noted other officers turning to glimpse at her before moving subtly out of her way.

Finally, she came to a glass door and opened it. "*Entrez,*" she said, and Michael stepped into the small office.

Schleck sat down at her desk and gestured for Michael to sit opposite. "Monsieur Farleigh tells me you were a priest."

Michael adjusted his glasses. There it was again. "Yes, that's right."

"And you're a PI now."

"Of a sort." Was he being interrogated? "Why did you leave the priesthood?"

Michael blinked. It was the first time anyone had asked him outright. He didn't want to answer and didn't have to as the door opened and a young officer entered; a solid woman with messy blonde hair and a crumpled uniform. She handed a file to Schleck and turned to Michael, smiling.

"You are investigating the Farleigh Case, *non*?" Slightly out of breath, her voice and rosy cheeks conveyed heightened enthusiasm. The officer's hair was even messier from the front, and a sprinkling of crumbs adorned her shirt.

Michael nodded. "I am here on behalf of the family to—"

"*C'est tout,* Georgette. *Merci,*" Schleck commanded, then snapped open the file and jotted a note.

Georgette scratched her hair, shrugged her shoulders at Michael and left the office.

Schleck looked up, her grey eyes assessing him from under two perfectly manicured eyebrows. "So, you left the priesthood because—?"

"Ah – I left for personal reasons."

Awkward silence filled the office as Schleck finished writing in the file. "I see," she muttered. "I myself am Catholic."

"Oh," Michael managed.

"So, you have questions?" She put the pen down and leaned back in her chair, looking at him with one of those perfect eyebrows arched.

Michael cleared his throat. "Well, as you know I am here on behalf of the Farleighs to investigate what happened to Emma. I was wondering if you would tell me what you found."

"We sent the Farleighs a summary of the evidence."

"Yes, and they have passed it on to me. I wondered why you stopped investigating after just a month."

Schleck pursed her lips. "Inspecteur Roulier is a genius with his work. I am efficient. I work our team hard and smart, Monsieur."

Michael believed her. The small office was neat and ordered, not one paper dared to shift out of place. Two filing cabinets stood to attention against one wall, a couple of shelves along another with journals and books, upright and perfectly aligned. Not a speck of dust to be seen. Only her coffee cup upset the balance – a hint of red lipstick had smeared near the rim.

"We collected all the evidence by the end of the first week. Every stone was upturned I can assure you. But the case ran cold. There was nothing more we could do. It seems Mademoiselle Farleigh eluded us all."

"You think she has – run away?"

Schleck plucked a tissue from a box on her desk and wiped the lipstick smudge off her cup. "That was our conclusion. She was a smart young woman. We believe she may have orchestrated her own disappearance." She threw the tissue in the empty waste paper basket and returned her attention to Michael.

"But why would she do that?"

Schleck pursed her lips again. "Perhaps her family put pressure on her to return. Her father was angry that she had been working in Paris at all."

Michael frowned. He'd detected the earl's displeasure about Emma's living in Paris, but was that enough to make Emma run away? "And, the file you gave to the Farleighs, it is comprehensive?"

Schleck blinked and looked to the side. "It is everything we can share, yes. We are confident in our conclusion of this case, Monsieur." She locked eyes with him again. "Emma Farleigh wanted to disappear. She was living an imaginary life and she left to pursue a fairytale world that she had dreamt up. It may be that she had a psychiatric illness. We have posted several alerts to authorities, including hospitals, throughout the country. If she is still in France there is a strong possibility that she will re-appear somewhere." She looked at her watch. "Now, if you have no more questions …"

"Of course." Michael stood. "Thank you for your time, Madame."

He walked back through the echoing corridor, wondering what it was Schleck hadn't told him.

Chapter Three
Excerpt from Michael D'Angelo's case notes

Tuesday 18th November

Met with Detective Schleck today. She wasn't exactly a barrel of laughs, not that I expected a comedian. I wish Inspector Roulier had been available. Perhaps he'd be more forthcoming. Schleck added no further information to what I have already gleaned from the summary of evidence. But I can't help feeling she withheld something.

Tomorrow I will meet with two of Emma's work colleagues – John, a fellow Englishman, and Anais, a French native who has worked in the States. In the blog Emma called them 'Jack' and 'Amelie'. Hopefully they can reveal something more than what's in the police notes.

NB – I keep thinking about vampires. Obvious, considering Emma's blog. But, I'm sure I came across some pearl of wisdom about them years ago. Perhaps I should contact Patrick at the Athenaeum. He was one of the few who didn't judge me, and his knowledge of demonology was good.

THERE WERE FEW TOURISTS ENTERING THE LOUVRE, AND Michael was grateful for that. It would have been more difficult for John to find him during peak season. The glass panes of the Louvre's famous pyramid reflected the steel sky above. Michael squinted, wondering if it was possible to count them to confirm or deny the urban legend that it contained exactly 666 panels. A cool breeze tousled his hair and he rubbed his gloved hands together.

"Monsieur D'Angelo?"

Michael turned and a bearded man with dark hair approached. "*Oui*."

"John." The man extended his hand and Michael shook it.

"Thank you for meeting me."

John shrugged as he unbuttoned a shirt pocket, extracting a packet of cigarettes. "I'd like to help." He lit a smoke and exhaled.

Michael tried not to cough.

"Emma's a good girl. Innocent." John shook his head. "If only she'd told me." His accent revealed his heritage – English, from the north.

Michael adjusted his glasses. "Told you?"

John took another puff, nodding. "The whole translation business. The blog. I'da talked her outta it."

"Perhaps that's why she didn't tell you."

John finished his cigarette as he led Michael through the few ambling tourists, under the glass pyramid and down stairs, through halls and up stairs until they came to a room with two small windows and shelves, floor to ceiling, filled with books, boxes and crates. Along the window sat two desks both messy with files, old coffee cups and stationery, but one notably more chaotic than the other. John pulled up the desk chairs.

"Have a seat."

"This is Emma's office, too?"

John pointed to the slightly more ordered desk. "That's hers. Still no replacement for her." He ran a hand through his dark hair and leaned back on the chair. "My work's doubled since all this."

"Tell me about Emma's work."

"Emma and I are conservators; we work with old books mostly."

"They have books in the Louvre?" Michael looked up; he was pretty sure the Louvre galleries sat above them somewhere.

"No. They shove us here so we can use the expensive lab." He nodded to a door between the bulging shelves. "The Louvre has connections with other museums, galleries and universities throughout the world. So our efforts can end up anywhere." He scratched his beard. "It's not a bad place to work. Gets annoying in peak tourist season though."

"Two English people working in this tiny office in the middle of Paris."

John laughed. "We got on, Emma and me, once she put me in my place." He winked.

"So you're 'Jack' in the blog. She also talks of Philippe and Amelie." Michael opened his tablet to the case notes.

"By Philippe she meant Pascal, our gaffer. He's a hard taskmaster and misses little, but we both consider him a bit of a prat. Full of himself. Amelie is Anais. She works here and was good friends with Emma. They spent time together on weekends, shopping and all that girly crap. I'll call her, just a tick." John picked up the phone and dialled, speaking swiftly in French. It was almost like another voice, so different from his northern accent.

"She'll be here in a min."

Michael opened a new page of notes and typed the date '19th November' and John's name. "So according to Emma's blog, you came across the diary first?"

"Ah, that bloody thing. It was found after a fire, just like she wrote in the blog." "You've read the blog?"

"The whole of bloody France read it, mate! The media had a bloody field day with it. Juicy story like that."

"I see."

"Poor Em. Old world stuff really grabbed her. You read some

weird shite in our job. People in history were fucked up. 'Scuse the language."

"Please, not on my account."

John looked out the small window at two pigeons circling the concrete. "That diary ... Pascal asked me to do a quick assessment. We were already bogged down by a shitload of other artefacts out of a dig up Normandy way. He wanted to know if it was worth our time. Emma was right. I was too quick in my assessment. All I did was scan the pages to read some crazy shite in it." He ran a hand through his beard. "I've been in this business for longer than Em and I've seen a few fakes in my time. This one smacked of it. The whole thing was a bloody joke. I decided it wasn't a priority and put it aside. But Em ..." He shook his head. "She had her heart set on it. Her big bloody eyes were all over it. Ah! I shouldn't have let her have it."

The door opened and a young woman stepped into the office. Her blond hair had a streak of pink and was tied up in a loose bun atop her head. She wore red, thick-framed glasses with lipstick to match and her tight-fitting dress was an explosion of colour.

"*Bonjour*."

"*Bonjour.*" John stood and kissed her cheeks either side in the French fashion. "Anais, this is Michael D'Angelo."

Anais shook his hand and smiled. Michael could see she wasn't as young as he had originally thought; a woman in her thirties, perhaps. "*Enchanté*," Michael replied, softly.

Anais giggled, pushed a pile of files off the corner of John's desk, and parked her bottom. "So, you are an *investigateur* of the paranormal, *non?*" Her eyes gleamed. Her English held a faint American accent, no doubt a result of her time working in San Francisco. Michael had read that in the case notes.

He patted down the cowlick at the back of his hair. "Ah, well ..."

"I've googled you, monsieur! And you were a priest. How exciting!" She clapped her hands together.

"Really? A priest? Shite, sorry about the swearing, Father." John looked genuinely regretful.

Michael raised his hand and shook his head. "Please."

"So you think he really is a vampire? This mysterious Nathaniel? That's what the blog suggests." She leaned forward, seeming to wait with bated breath for his reply.

Michael adjusted his glasses. "Well, I am only just beginning my investigation—"

"You do!" Her mascara-lined eyes burned through her lenses into his very mind, it seemed. "You do think he's a vampire! I knew it." She jumped up and clapped again.

"Well, I might ask you a few questions about him?" He wondered if she had some power to read people's subconsciousness. Did he believe this idea of vampires after all? What was that thing he couldn't remember? Could she tell him that, too? He cleared his throat. "About Nathaniel. I understand you were the only other person in Emma's life who saw him."

Anais's shoulders slouched and she sat down on the corner of the desk again, her excitement suddenly gone.

"*Oui*, that is correct." She took her glasses off and patted the corners of each eye.

"I am sorry." Michael's voice retained the softness of the confessional, a skill he was thankful for at times like this.

"It is all right." Anais sniffed, putting her glasses back on. "I am happy to answer your questions, *Père*."

"Please call me Michael. I am no longer a priest."

Anais's eyes seemed to turn a deal sadder. "Of course, Michael."

Michael knew the question that lingered in the forefront of her mind and he wanted to divert the conversation away from that quickly. "Did you have the opportunity to talk with this Nathaniel?"

Anais shook her head. "I did not meet him. I only saw him the night Emma first came across him at the Gypsy Bar. He was very handsome, dark shiny hair."

"All the handsome ones have dark hair." John winked and Anais ruffled his crop of dark waves.

"Of course they do, John." She smiled. "He had smouldering looks, and he was tall and strong-looking. The type of dark handsome stranger us girls fantasise about."

Michael shifted on his seat and adjusted his glasses again.

"You'll have to excuse her frankness, Michael," John said. "French women are more free with their fantasies than their British sisters."

"Ah, of course." Michael cleared his throat again. "Did you hear him speak at all? Did you catch anything of his conversation with Emma that night?"

"No," Anais replied. "I had found my own company by that stage."

Michael nodded and added a note to his tablet.

"I only glanced their way now and then. I am sorry. I'm probably not very much help. I wish I could help more. I miss Em."

"It's all right," Michael said, his voice soft again. "Perhaps there is something you observed that you have not considered as important. Some small detail that you noted that night that blended with everything else?"

Anais frowned. "What do you mean?"

"Perhaps if you closed your eyes?" "Close my eyes?"

Michael nodded. "Sometimes it helps to concentrate, to allow your mind to focus on the memory of him. You could describe him again – how he looks and maybe some small detail lodged in your memory will reveal itself."

Anais looked at John, who winked. "Don't worry. I'll make sure the priest doesn't have his way with you."

Anais gave him a light smack on his head. "Don't be cheeky!"

Michael finished a note on his tablet and squirmed in his seat again. Flirts made him uncomfortable.

"Okay." Anais nodded. "I will close my eyes if you think it will help."

Michael stood and put the tablet on his chair. "Would you mind if I put my palm on your forehead?"

Anais smiled. "I don't mind. But why?"

"It's hard to explain. It can help people to focus sometimes."

She shrugged. "Sure." And she closed her eyes.

Michael reached out and put his hand on her forehead and the other rested on her shoulder. He closed his own eyes and took a deep breath. It was time to access his gift, that secret part of his mind that would allow him to see what others could not. "Now, go back to that memory, that night at the club. When you first saw him, what were you doing?" His voice grew stronger, deeper. It always morphed a little when he did this.

Anais took a deep breath, too. "I waited at the bar. I turned around to smile at Em. He stood a small distance behind her. Then he approached our table."

"Catch that moment." The images were blurry, but with effort he could make them clearer. Michael pressed his hand more firmly to her forehead and concentrated. "Tell me what you see."

"He is tall. It is dark and gloomy, but I can see he is very handsome. His hair is groomed and slick. He's wearing a black jacket, even though it is quite warm in the bar. He wears a black silk shirt underneath."

An image of Nathaniel formed like a reflection in a pool of water. Michael shivered. "Where is he looking?"

Anais tried to turn her head but Michael gripped her forehead more firmly, his hand growing hotter still. "There's a man, oh!" She gasped. "It's the man who I met! Nathaniel was looking at him."

"Where is the man?"

"He's at the end of the bar. I can see his reflection in the mirror. He is ordering drinks."

"Good. You're doing very well, Anais. Now, play the memory again, slowly. What happens next?"

Anais's forehead warmed, but Michael maintained his hold. *Just a little longer*, he thought.

"The bartender, she gives me a drink, and tells me it is from the man at the end of the bar. I look at him and he smiles at me. I smile back and lift the drink to him. He walks over to me and asks my name. I tell him it is Anais and he tells me my eyes are like emeralds."

Michael frowned. The compliment bore similarity to those Nathaniel himself had paid Emma during their courtship, as documented in the blog. "Keep playing the memory, slowly. What else do you notice about him?"

Anais frowned under his hand. "He has light hair, blue eyes, very handsome. He's young. Much younger than I thought at the time, but his words sound very old. Too old for such a boy. He smiles at me – a lot. I look back at Emma then."

"What do you see?" Michael tightened his grip even further, his palm was burning now.

"Him, Nathaniel. He is with her, at our table. They are talking. I turn back and the man who bought me a drink, he is looking at them. Oh, my!" Anais took a sharp gasp and stood away, her eyes opened and her forehead was red as though she had been standing in the sun for too long. Her eyes wide with fear, mouth open.

"Anais? You all right?" John stood and reached for her. "Michael? What's going on?"

Michael shook the heat from his hand and caught his own breath. Her memory had been strong and its visioning had taken a lot of energy; he would need to rest soon. "She will be all right. I'm sorry. Sometimes this process is physically tiring."

Anais' hands shook as they went to her cheeks, and she whispered, "Mon Dieu!

Mon Dieu!"

"What's wrong? Michael? What's happening here?" John looked at him with a frown.

"Anais." Michael's voice had reverted to the soft tone of the confessional. "Now breathe easily and tell us what you saw. What has made you so upset?"

She inhaled slowly and closed her eyes. Michael sensed her calm. She opened her eyes again. "The man, the one who bought me a drink?"

"Yes?" Michael encouraged.

"He had a small wound on his neck. Very faint, almost healed but I saw it clearly."

Michael frowned. "Go on."

"There were two small pricks. Just like she said in her blog. Two small red puncture wounds on the side of his neck."

Visit Amazon now to continue reading.

If you enjoy Aderyn Wood's stories you may like to read more of her work and also be informed of new releases and special discounts. Sign up to Aderyn's monthly newsletter today and you will receive a book of your choice for free.

THE EARL'S DAUGHTER

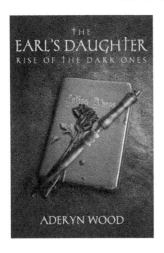

"Find out what kind of monster his is, and bring my daughter back to us."

Michael D'Angelo doesn't normally investigate murder, but since they never found Emma's body, she's technically just a missing person. But he doesn't investigate those either.

After the Earl of Wolston reads the translation of a sinister and ancient text published on his daughter's blog, in the days leading up to her disappearance, he reaches out to Mr D'Angelo, convinced that evil forces are at work: something beyond the ordinary, something not of this world, something unholy.

Fortunately for Michael, Paranormal Investigations are his specialty. But as Michael unravels Emma's last days, and the secrets inscribed on her blog, strange new entities reveal themselves, and he begins to question whether such knowledge is too dangerous to pursue.

THE PHARAOH'S MISTRESS

"But vampires don't dream. Do they?"

Emma and Michael escaped the slayer's castle, but the vampire hunter pursues them in earnest, determined to use Emma as bait to draw out a much bigger fish – the oldest and most powerful vampire on Earth.

But something else draws Emma east and it calls to her in human-like dreams. As the mysterious pull heightens, Emma's new vampire instincts grow increasingly erratic. Michael suffers his own demons and the longer he stays with Emma the more difficult it becomes to resist certain desires of the flesh.

As they race deeper into the desert, a brush with Emma's maker – the infamous viscount's son, Nathaniel Chartley; along with Michael's new chum, Georgette, reveals that they may be on the cusp of the end of days.

It will mean the end for someone – slayer, vampire or human?

An entire species is about to die out.

THE RAVEN – THE SECRET CHRONICLES OF LOST MAGIC

***Clan of the Cave Bear* meets Epic Fantasy...**

The clan's survival is under threat, but one has the power to save them – their Outcast.

In the Wolf Clan, in winter's darkest hour, a baby is born with a powerful gift. But dangerous omens brand her an Outcast, and the Elders name her Iluna.

As Iluna comes of age, dark magic, war, and treachery soon jeopardize the life of every clan member; many suspect Iluna and her gift. Is she to blame? Or is she salvation?

Iluna must decide: save the clan, or save herself.

'The Secret Chronicles of Lost Magic' is a collection of standalone epic fantasy novels rather than a series. Each novel is a complete story that invites readers to fully immerse into a rich fantasy world. Each 'Chronicle' is set in a different era within the same world and can be read in any order, but here's the chronology for interested readers:

#1 The Raven – a 'prehistoric' era

#2 Dragonshade – a 'Bronze Age' era

DRAGONSHADE – THE SECRET CHRONICLES OF LOST MAGIC

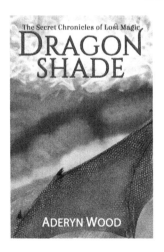

***This* game of thrones will be played by gods. And when the gods play, ancient cities burn...**

Prince Sargan is the worst swordsman in all Zraemia. His clumsy performance draws scorn from his uncle, pity from his sister, disappointment from his father, and sniggers from everyone else.

But soon, Sargan will enter the temple and begin his long-awaited path to the seat of high priest.

His brother will one day inherit the throne.

His sister will marry.

The enemy king will leave them alone.

And all will be right with the world.

Unless... the gods change the game.

And when the gods play, the game turns to war – the Great War.

Ancient prophecies surface, dark enemies rise, new allies emerge, old ones can't be trusted, magic scorches the earth, reluctant heroes are made, and nothing is ever the same again.

'The Secret Chronicles of Lost Magic' is a collection of standalone epic fantasy novels rather than a series. Each novel is a complete story that invites readers to fully immerse into a rich fantasy world. Each 'Chronicle' is set in a different era within the same world and can be read in any order, but here's the chronology for interested readers:

#1 The Raven – a 'prehistoric' era

#2 Dragonshade – a 'Bronze Age' era

THE BORDERLANDS TRILOGY

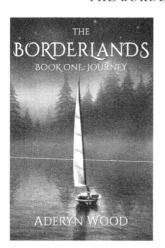

Dale has never felt a sense of belonging. She despises the bullies and snobs at school, and her family are difficult to like, let alone love. Rhys, a new boy at school seems to take an interest in her. But can she trust him? When the only friend she has ever had, Old Man Gareth, is murdered before her eyes, she is set on a frantic journey and a lonely adventure; the Borderlands beckon. But what are the Borderlands? Will she make it to them? And if she gets there, will she belong?

The Borderlands: Journey is a magical fantasy adventure that fantasy fiction fans, particularly older teens and the young at heart, will enjoy. It is the first book in the Contemporary Fantasy series 'The Borderlands'.

ABOUT THE AUTHOR

From high fantasy to paranormal, Aderyn's stories cover the broad spectrum of Fantasy. Inspired from childhood by the wonder and mystique of Susan Cooper's *The Dark is Rising* and the adventures in Tolkien's *The Hobbit*, her love of the Fantasy genre has been life long. As a writer, Aderyn brings characters and places to life in stories filled with magic, mystery, and a good dollop of mayhem.

Aderyn studied Literature, History and Creative Writing at university, travelled the world, and taught English before becoming a full-time writer. She is also a part-time farmer passionate about self-sufficiency and poultry. She lives in a cosy cottage on a small farm in Victoria, Australia with partner Peter, their dog, cat, and a little duck called Snow.

If you'd like to be informed of the next installment in the *The Viscount's Son* trilogy consider subscribing to Aderyn's newsletter.

www.aderynwood.com

Made in the USA
Monee, IL
04 December 2020

50895127R00046